Camille

Carlos

Ribbon Road

Beachside Boulevard

Long Lane

Police Station

Readalot Library

Squiggly Street

Stay and Play Park

Friendly Waves Beach

Gym and Swim Recreation Center

Duck Duck Goose Pond

School Street

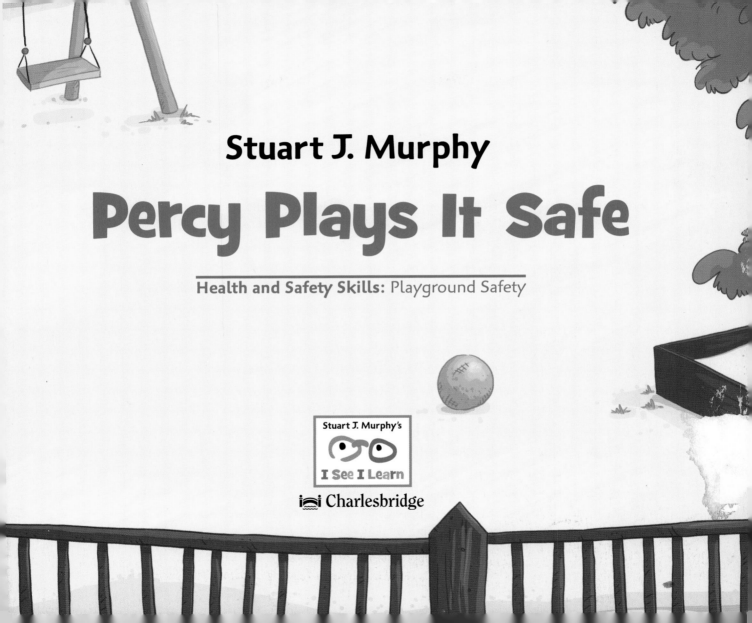

Stuart J. Murphy

Percy Plays It Safe

Health and Safety Skills: Playground Safety

Stuart J. Murphy's

I See I Learn

ini Charlesbridge

Percy went to the playground almost every day.

There were slides and swings,

monkey bars and slippery poles,

and even a great big sandbox.

Percy played on everything.
But sometimes Percy didn't play safe.

Sometimes he was a monster.

"Rrrroar!" roared Percy as he swung on the monkey bars. He almost bumped into Freda.

"**Watch out!**" she said.

"Grrrrrr," Percy growled as he crawled up the slide.
"Hey!" called Ajay.

Percy flew down headfirst.
"**Stop!**" shouted Camille.

"Monsters never stop!" yelled Percy.
He ran through the sandbox.

"It's no fun to play with you!" hollered Freda.
"**Play safe**," Percy's daddy called out,
"or we'll have to go home."

But Percy kept going.
He jumped onto a swing.

He pumped and pumped.

Then he jumped off . . .

and landed right on his knee.

"OWWWW!" screamed Percy.

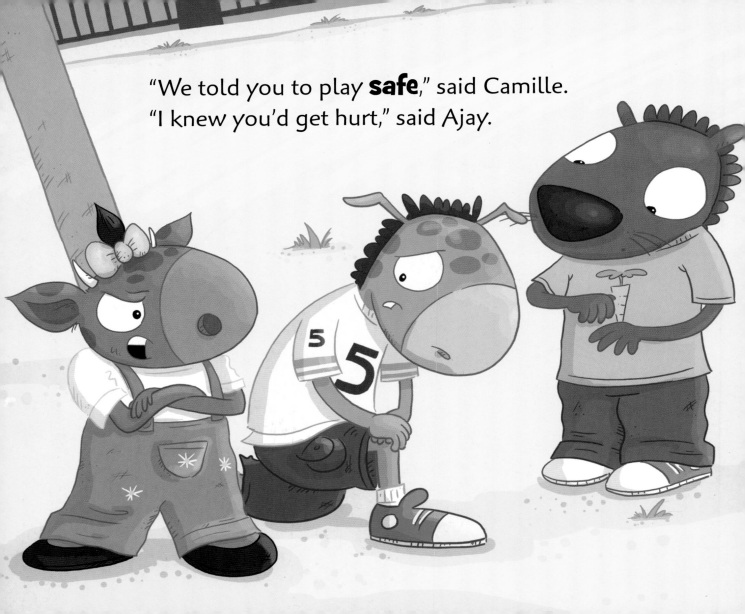

"We told you to play **safe**," said Camille.
"I knew you'd get hurt," said Ajay.

"I'll get your daddy," said Freda.

The next day Percy came back.
He slid on the slide and played in the sandbox.
He even swung on the swings.

"We're **safe** monsters, too," said Freda.
Then, all together, Freda, Ajay, Camille,
and Percy made the biggest roar ever.

A Closer Look

1. How do **you** play safe?

2. Look at the pictures of Percy playing.
   When is he playing in a safe way?

3. When is Percy playing in an unsafe way?
   Why is it unsafe?

4. What are some good rules for safe play?

5. Pretend you are Percy.
   Act out how he played in a safe way.

A Note About Visual Learning and Young Children

Visual Learning describes how we gather and process information from illustrations, diagrams, graphs, symbols, photographs, icons, and other visual models. Long before children can read—or even speak many words—they are able to assimilate visual information with ease. By the time they reach pre-kindergarten age (3–5), they are accomplished visual learners.

I SEE I LEARN™ books build on this natural talent, using inset pictures, diagrams, and highlighted words to help reinforce lessons conveyed through simple stories. The series covers social, emotional, health and safety, and cognitive skills.

Percy Plays It Safe focuses on playground safety. Knowing how to follow playground rules, using common sense, and respecting one another are important to keep children from hurting themselves or others.

Safe play is fun play!

 Stuart